Wicked Wolf Tales

WicKed WOLF TaleS

Retold by Laura CeCil

ILLUSTrated by

EMMa CHiCHeSter CLarK

PAVILION

For Finn
E.C.C.

For Edmund
L.C.

First published in Italy by Arnoldo Mondadori Editore S.p.A., in 1999
under the title *Cappuccetto Rosso e altre storie di lupi cattivi*

First published in Great Britain in 2001 by
PAVILION BOOKS LIMITED
London House, Great Eastern Wharf
Parkgate Road, London SW11 4NQ
www.pavilionbooks.co.uk

Designed by Ness Wood at Zoom Design

A CIP catalogue record for this book is available
from the British Library.

ISBN 1 86205 460 6

Set in Bell MT
Printed and bound in Singapore by Kyodo
Colour origination by AGP Repro (UK) Ltd.

2 4 6 8 10 9 7 5 3 1

This book can be ordered direct from the publisher. Please contact
the Marketing Department. But try your bookshop first.

Contents

Little Red Riding Hood

Little Red Riding Hood

The Wicked Wolf

The Wicked Wolf and the Seven Little Kids

Berta

The Wicked Wolf

Ben   **Babs**   **Bette**   **Bob**   **Billy**   **Bonny**   **Bertie**

Mr W. Wolf

Daisy

Mr W. Wolf

Introduction

I always loved reading aloud to my children when they were small, because it was a chance to share stories that enthralled and amused them, while I could indulge myself by acting out the different characters. My parents often read to me and my earliest memories are of hearing stories like *Little Red Riding Hood* and joining in with "All the better to eat you with, my dear!"

So this collection is designed to make reading aloud as much fun for the reader as for the listener. The retelling concentrates on direct speech, with opportunities for different voices and repeated phrases so that children can join in, rather than on description. In any case, Emma's illustrations provide this – you can tell by looking at Mr W. Wolf that you shouldn't trust him, or that Berta the goat will try to save her kids.

The book also uses distinctive type styles to suggest sound effects, dramatic moments and different voices in order to add variety and expression to reading aloud. This also helps young children beginning to read. All reading starts as reading aloud, and it is much easier to learn words and phrases if you can associate them with sounds and expressions.

About the Tales

Little Red Riding Hood and *The Wicked Wolf and the Seven Little Kids* will be familiar to most people, but *Mr W. Wolf* is a humorous Italian folktale that deserves to be better-known.

Little Red Riding Hood

One bright sunny morning a little girl was playing in the garden when her mother called from the house:

"Little Red Riding Hood, where are you? It is time for you to visit your granny."

Red Riding Hood ran happily to her mother. She loved visiting her granny. She always gave Red Riding Hood sweets, and let her rock in her rocking chair. Granny also told her wonderful stories.

Little Red Riding Hood enjoyed the walk to her granny's house, because the path went by a stream where she could pick blackberries.

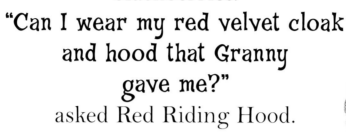

"Can I wear my red velvet cloak and hood that Granny gave me?" asked Red Riding Hood.

"You won't need it. It's much too warm," answered her mother. But Red Riding Hood adored her cloak and wore it whenever she could. **This was the reason why everyone called her Red Riding Hood.**

"Mama," said Little Red Riding Hood, "I will run all the way to Granny's house."

"No, don't do that," said Mama. "In the basket there are **two loaves, fresh cheese** and **a pot of jam** for Granny. If you fall, you will break everything."

"Off you go now and don't dawdle, don't speak to strangers and don't stop at the stream..."

But before Mama could finish, Little Red Riding Hood went skipping off along the path to her grandmother's house.

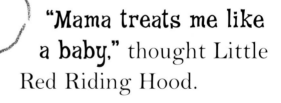

"Mama treats me like a baby," thought Little Red Riding Hood.

"Don't do this, don't do that.
OOH, what lovely blackberries!
I will pick some for Granny."

Little Red Riding Hood put the basket on
the ground and started to fill her
pockets with the delicious fruit.

"How strange," said Little Red Riding Hood,
"the birds aren't singing today and
where are all the squirrels?"
But Little Red Riding Hood did not know that all
the animals had hidden, because an unwelcome visitor
had just arrived...

15

In fact, the visitor was a **Wicked Wolf** and he was asleep behind the blackberry bushes at that very moment. Now the little girl's high voice woke him up.

The Wicked Wolf stretched and yawned. His mouth was so wide, it seemed as big as a cave.

Suddenly he appeared from behind the bushes.
"Good day, little girl," he said smoothly.
"Good day, sir," answered Red Riding Hood politely.
"What are you doing here?" asked the
Wicked Wolf.
"I am going to my granny's house to take her
some **bread, fresh cheese** and **jam**."

"Hmm... How delicious," said the Wicked Wolf.
Then with a gleam in his eye he asked: "And tell
me, are you on your way to Granny all on your own?"
"Yes, I am," answered Red Riding Hood.

"Hmmm... And does your granny live alone?"
The Wicked Wolf made a habit of eating children and
he was dying to gobble up this little girl. But he was afraid
a huntsman might see him if he ate her beside the stream.

So he planned to trick Little Red Riding Hood. Even if
grandmothers were not his favourite food, he said to himself,
"Two mouthfuls are better than one..."

"Does Granny live far away?" he asked innocently.

"Just at the end of this path, in the yellow cottage with the wooden roof."

"Fantastic!" said the Wicked Wolf. "Listen, I must hurry away now. But you carry on picking blackberries from my bush."

"Is this bush yours, sir?" asked Little Red Riding Hood in surprise.

"Yes!" lied the Wolf. "But don't worry, I don't like blackberries. You stay here and enjoy this beautiful sunny day."

19

"You are very kind. Thank you so much," said Little Red Riding Hood.

The Wicked Wolf was a coward as well as a liar, so as he went he called out: "Is your grandmother very strong?"

"Oh no, sir, she is quite weak because she has been ill," replied Little Red Riding Hood.

"Weak!" the Wolf gloated, "Better still!" Little Red Riding Hood went on picking blackberries along the path beside the stream for quite a time.

"Mama was right, it really is hot," she thought suddenly. "I'll just cool off in the water for a moment, before I visit Granny." Little Red Riding Hood took off her cloak, her shoes and her socks, and paddled in the stream. The cool water was so refreshing that the moment became half an hour.

Meanwhile, the Wicked Wolf had arrived at Granny's house. He approached the door cautiously. "Hmm... Let's see ... end of the path, yellow house, wooden roof... Yes, this must be it."
He found the door open because Granny already knew that Little Red Riding Hood was coming.

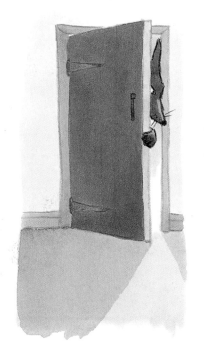

"May I come in?"
said the
Wicked Wolf.

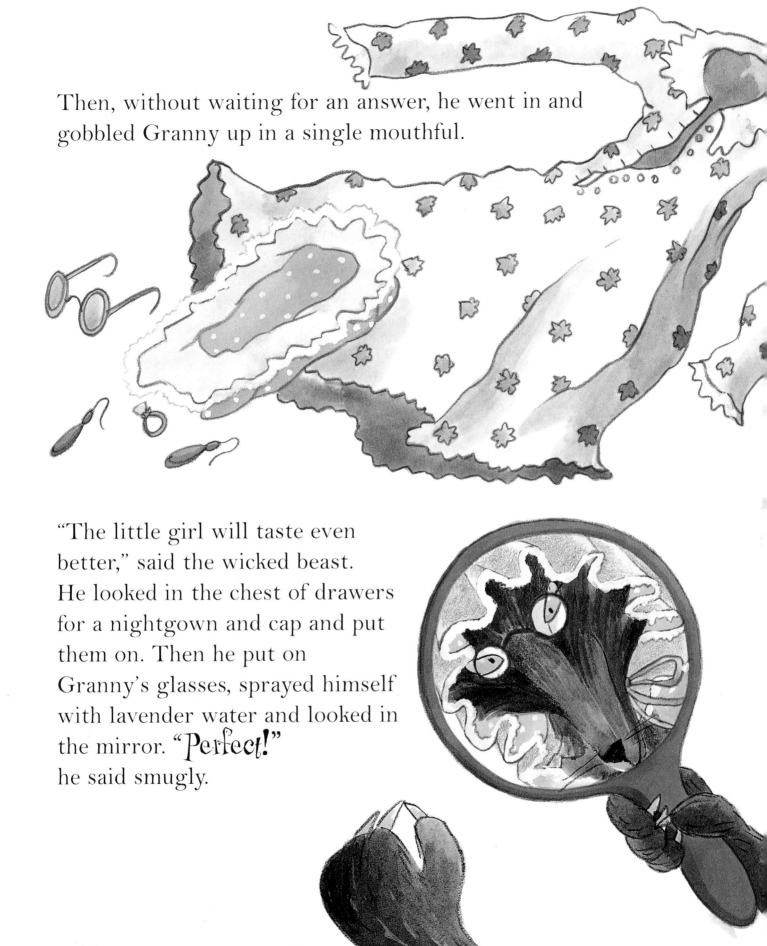

Then, without waiting for an answer, he went in and gobbled Granny up in a single mouthful.

"The little girl will taste even better," said the wicked beast. He looked in the chest of drawers for a nightgown and cap and put them on. Then he put on Granny's glasses, sprayed himself with lavender water and looked in the mirror. "Perfect!" he said smugly.

He had just had time to climb
between the sheets when he heard
Little Red Riding Hood's voice.
"It's me, Granny!" she said, and
came into the bedroom.

"Hello, sweetheart," said the Wolf,
trying to imitate Granny's quavering
voice. "Come and sit on the bed
next to me." His eyes flashed with
a terrible gleam.

"Guess what lovely things I've brought you, Granny," said Little Red Riding Hood. "**Two loaves, fresh cheese** and **a pot of jam,** and look at this! Blackberries! I picked them for you on the way here..."

But suddenly Little Red Riding Hood stopped talking
and looked more closely at her grandmother's face.
"Goodness me, Granny! What big ears you've
got today!"
"All the better to hear you with,
my dear," said the Wicked Wolf.

"And what big eyes you've
got!" said Red Riding Hood.
"All the better to see you
with, my dear!" said the
Wicked Wolf.

"And... Oh, Granny! What huge
hairy hands you have!" said
Little Red Riding Hood, staring
at her grandmother in surprise.
"All the better to hold you
with, my dear," said the
Wicked Wolf, his mouth
watering.

Little Red Riding Hood looked at the Wolf silently, then she said once more, "Oh, Granny, I don't understand! What an enormous cavernous mouth you've got."

"All the better to eat you with!" growled the Wicked Wolf.

He leapt at her with
his mouth open wide.
But his legs got
twisted up in Granny's
long nightgown, and
Little Red Riding
Hood dodged away.
SNIP SNAP went his
huge jaws just behind
her as she ran.

Snarling with rage, the Wicked Wolf pulled off Granny's clothes and went after her.

"Help! Help! Save me from the Wicked Wolf!" screamed Little
Red Riding Hood.
Only just in time, a huntsman heard her cries. With his great
gun he shot the Wicked Wolf.

Poor Little Red Riding Hood burst into tears. "Where is my granny?" she cried.

"If I know that wolf," said the huntsman, "he will have eaten her in one gulp. She may still be alive inside him."

Then he cut open the Wicked Wolf, and there was
Granny – all in one piece!
"Thank goodness we are both safe," said Granny.
"After all that, I'm as hungry as the Wolf. What nice
things have you brought me?"
So they ate the two loaves, fresh cheese and the pot
of jam and blackberries, and Little Red Riding Hood
promised that from now on she would always do as
her mother told her.

THE WICKED WOLF
and the
SEVEN LITTLE KIDS

This is a story about a goat called Berta and her seven little kids.

The first kid was called **Ben** and he was white.

The second was called **Bette** and she was black.

The third was called **Billy** and he was black with white spots.

The fourth was called **Bonny** and she was white with black spots.

The fifth was called **Bob** and he was dark brown.

The sixth was called **Babs** and she was brown with white spots.

And the seventh was called **Bertie** and he was coffee-coloured.

One day Berta told her kids she must go to the market. "You are old enough to stay on your own," she said.

"But don't open the door to anyone. If the Wicked Wolf came in, he would gobble you up in one gulp. He is very cunning. Sometimes he wears a disguise so you won't know him."

"Be good and don't quarrel. Don't eat too much chocolate — you know it gives you a tummy ache — and don't jump on the beds with dirty hooves. Above all, don't open the door to anybody. Do you understand? Not to ANYBODY — especially the Wicked Wolf. I won't be long and I'll bring back something nice."

She said goodbye and left the house. Once they were alone, the kids decided to play 'wolf hide-and-seek'.

Bertie played the wolf while the others ran and hid.

Billy climbed into the stove.

Bette ran under the table.

When **Bertie** had counted up to a hundred, he howled like a wolf and began to look for his brothers and sisters.

He looked in the saucepans, he lifted up the tablecloth and searched under the chairs until he had found them all.

"Now it's **Bette's** turn to be wolf," said **Bertie** who had an idea for a special hiding place.

But just at that moment someone knocked on the door.

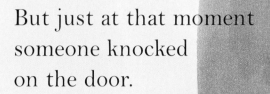

TAP TAP TAP

Immediately the kids were silent. **Who could it be?** "Open the door. It's your mama," said a low gruff voice. "I have brought a nice present for you all." "Well, you can keep it," answered **Ben** at once. "You're not our mother," said Bonnie. **"Our mother has a voice as sweet as milk and honey."** "But you have a low gruff voice," said **Bertie.** "You must be the Wicked Wolf. Go away!" "Yes, go away! Go away!" shouted the seven little kids.

The Wicked Wolf gnashed his teeth with rage and went away. "Ugly little brats!" he said. "If they want a sweet voice, well, then I'll give them a sweet voice..."
He went into a baker's shop and asked if they had any sweet cakes.

"Sweet cakes, sir," said the baker, "those are our speciality!"
The Wicked Wolf couldn't bear to eat sweet things, and was
revolted by the smell of sugary cakes and pastries. But he
gulped and asked for the sweetest cake in the shop. Then he
held his nose with one
paw, thrust the cake
down his throat and
ran back to the
little goats' house.

The Wicked Wolf knocked for a second time on the kids' door.

TAP TAP TAP

And in his new, sweet, sugary voice he said, "Open up, it is your mama. I've brought you all a lovely present."

"Could it be Mama?" said **Billy**.

"Better check," said **Bette** going to the door.

Through the keyhole she saw a black hairy leg.

"It's got black legs!" shrieked **Bette**.

"You're not our mother!" said **Babs**. "Our mother's legs are white as snow! You're the Wicked Wolf. Go away!"

"Yes, go away! Go away!" shouted the seven little kids.

For a second time the Wicked Wolf went away.
He was furious. He went to the miller
and asked for a bag of flour.
"What are you going to use the flour for?"
the miller asked suspiciously.
"I need it to make bread, and I'm very
hungry," said the Wicked Wolf.
    "Be quick or else I will eat you!"
        The terrified miller got the bag of
            flour. The Wicked Wolf opened it and
            thrust his paws inside. When his legs
            were thoroughly white, he ran off.

So for the third time that morning the Wicked Wolf knocked on the door of the little goats' house.

TAP TAP TAP "Open up, my darlings, it's Mama with a present for you all," said the Wicked Wolf in his sugary voice. He put a white paw up to the keyhole and added...

"Don't you recognize me? I am your mother with a voice as sweet as milk and honey, and legs as bla— ahem, as white as snow."

When **Babs** looked through the keyhole
she saw some white hair.
"She's got white legs!" she said.
"And she's got a sweet voice!"
added **Ben.**
"It must be Mama!"
exclaimed the seven little kids
at once,
running to
unlock
the door.
The door
flew
open.

A gust of cold air blew into the room, the little goats jumped
with fear – for there in front of them stood *the Wicked Wolf!*

"The Wicked Wolf! The Wicked Wolf!" shrieked the seven little kids in terror. **"Run and hide!"** And **Bette** ran under the table, **Ben** under the armchair, **Billy** into the stove, **Bonny** behind the curtains, **Bob** into the cupboard and **Babs** under the sink. **Bertie hid** in the grandfather clock which was his special hiding place. "It's no use running away," said the Wolf. *"I'll find all of you in the end."*

The Wicked Wolf looked under the table, under the armchair, inside the stove, behind the curtains, inside the cupboard, under the sink, and he swallowed up each of the little kids in one gulp. All except **Bertie**. The Wicked Wolf went on looking for him. He looked again under the chair, behind the curtains, under the sink… Then he heard a strange noise.

THUMP THUMP THUMP

It was the little goat's heart beating loudly with fear. The Wolf put his ear to the grandfather clock, smiled and said, "It's only this ticking thing."

"Oh well, I've eaten enough for today. I'll do without the seventh little kid." Then he went outside to lie down under a nearby tree. A short time later **Berta** returned. She found the door unlocked and the house deserted. When she saw the chair overturned, the curtains torn and the table broken, she knew what had happened. One after another she called her little kids. But nobody answered. Suddenly **Berta** heard **Bertie** crying out.

"The Wolf tricked us, Mama," explained **Bertie** between his sobs. "He did some magic and his voice became sweet and his legs white, so we opened the door because we believed he was you. And when we saw he was the Wicked Wolf we ran to hide, but he ate everybody except me."

"The scoundrel!" said **Berta**. But **Berta** did not lose heart. She took a pair of

huge scissors,

a needle and thread

and her sewing glasses

and put them all in her apron pocket.

"Oh Mama," said **Bertie**, "what do we do now?"

"Now it's our turn to trick the Wicked Wolf," said **Berta**.

The Wicked Wolf wasn't hard to find. He was stretched out, fast asleep, snoring loudly.

Berta took the huge scissors and slowly, slowly began to cut open the Wicked Wolf's stomach. One by one the six little kids jumped out. They were all alive and well! But there was no time to lose before the Wicked Wolf woke up.

"Hurry!" said **Berta**. "Bring me all the stones you can find." Quickly the little goats did as they were told. **Berta** filled the Wolf's stomach with the stones, then sewed it up as fast as she could.

When the Wicked Wolf woke up he felt very thirsty. "Those little kids were delicious, but perhaps I ate too many," he said. "My stomach is groaning." And he began to sing:

"Six little goats today,
Six little goats I've gobbled,
The seventh one got away,
But tomorrow I'll have him nobbled."

Then the Wicked Wolf staggered to the stream and leant over to drink. But he was so heavy he toppled into the water and sank to the bottom.

From that day on, the kids and their mother lived peacefully and happily, although **Bertie** always remembered his special hiding place – just in case.

Mr W. Wolf

There was once a little girl called Daisy and she was very greedy.

She liked **chocolate.**

She loved **sweets.**

She was wild about **ice creams,** and crazy for **cream cakes,** but most of all she adored **sticky doughnuts.**

Daisy was bored by school, but one day her teacher brought in a large bag of home-made sticky doughnuts. "As soon as you have finished your work, we can share these," she said.

The teacher told the children to draw a picture of the poem they had read. The poem described apple trees, and clouds in the autumn sky.

"What boring things!" Daisy grumbled.

She looked at her blank page and drew an enormous **sticky doughnut**. But that wasn't what her teacher wanted, so she quickly took more paper. She forced herself to think about clouds, but she drew them round, with holes in the middle, just like **doughnuts**! Next she drew the trees, but her apples looked just like huge **ice creams**.

So Daisy threw away the second drawing and asked the teacher if she could go to the sick room. "I'll stay in the corridor until it is time for the **doughnuts**," she said to herself.

She found somewhere to sit and soon fell fast asleep. While she slept, she had an amazing dream. She dreamt that her school had been turned into a wonderful shop full of mysterious coloured drawers. She had a little bell and every time she rang it the drawers opened.

And what do you think was in the drawers?
All kinds of sweets, chocolates, biscuits, cakes,
nougat and **sticky doughnuts.**
Daisy ran from drawer to drawer ringing her little
bell, and she tasted everything.
"Hurrah, Hurrah!" she squealed.

Ding! Ding! Ding!

Suddenly the bell for the end of school woke Daisy up. She remembered the **sticky doughnuts** and ran to the classroom. But she was already too late. Her classmates had eaten them all, and only left a few crumbs.

"Oh!" said Daisy's teacher. "We thought you were still feeling sick and wouldn't want anything to eat!"

Daisy was so disappointed. She ran crying to tell her mother. **"Mama!"** she bawled. "I went to the sick room and the others ate all the **sticky doughnuts** teacher brought for us. I didn't even get a tiny bit…"

"Don't cry, my love," said her mother. "I'll make you some **sticky doughnuts** which will taste even better. Come on now, let's go home."

But when they got home, Mama found that her frying pan had a large hole in it.

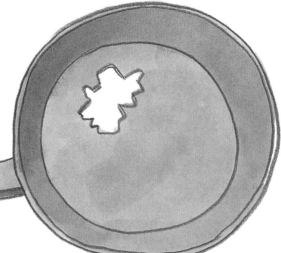

"Never mind," she said. "Go and borrow a frying pan from Mr W. Wolf."

Daisy was not keen to go. Mr W. Wolf lived on his own and people were scared of him. But she wanted **sticky doughnuts** more than anything. So she went to Mr Wolf's house and knocked on the door.

BOOM! BOOM!

"Who's that knocking on my door?" came a hollow voice from inside the house.

"It's me," said Daisy.

"Which me?" asked Mr Wolf. "Nobody ever comes here. What do you want?"

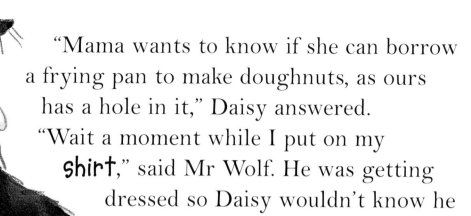

"Mama wants to know if she can borrow a frying pan to make doughnuts, as ours has a hole in it," Daisy answered.
"Wait a moment while I put on my **shirt**," said Mr Wolf. He was getting dressed so Daisy wouldn't know he was really a wolf.

But Daisy impatiently knocked again.

BOOM! BOOM!

"Wait a moment while I put on my **trousers**," said Mr Wolf.

BOOM! BOOM!

"Wait a moment while I put on my **jacket**," said Mr Wolf.

At last Mr W. Wolf opened the door.
"Here is the frying pan! But you must tell your mother to give it back to me full of her **sticky doughnuts.** Mmm ... with a good bottle of lemonade and a loaf of fresh bread. Is that clear?"

"I'll tell her, don't worry," Daisy answered, and she ran home. "Mama, Mr Wolf has lent us a frying pan, but in return he wants lemonade,

fresh bread

and doughnuts. What a cheek!"

"Don't be ungrateful," said
her mother. "We'll give Mr Wolf
everything he wants. Now help me
make these doughnuts."
She and Daisy set to work and
made them with jam, eggs
and sugar.

Then Daisy's mother put a heap of doughnuts on
one side. She put the rest in the pan and told
Daisy to take them to Mr Wolf with a bottle of
lemonade and a loaf of bread.
"Thank him for the pan. When you get back
we'll eat the doughnuts," said Mama.

But Daisy couldn't wait. As soon as she left the house she thought, "Suppose I try one doughnut? I don't think Mr Wolf would notice. After all, he only lent us the frying pan. I don't think it's fair of Mama to return it to him full of doughnuts, as well as bread and lemonade. I'll stop and try just one..."
But when Daisy had tasted the first doughnut, she couldn't stop.

One after another, she ate them all. She also drank the lemonade and gobbled up the loaf of bread. Finally there was not even a crumb left. "Help!" thought Daisy, "I must find something else to take to Mr Wolf!"

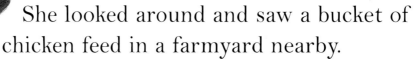

She looked around and saw a bucket of chicken feed in a farmyard nearby.

"I'll take some of that. Perhaps Mr Wolf has never eaten doughnuts and **so he won't know the difference."**

She took some of the chicken feed, rolled it into doughnut shapes and put them in the frying pan.

Then she went to the animals' drinking trough and filled the bottle with dirty water.

"Perhaps Mr Wolf has never drunk lemonade and **so he won't know the difference."**

She still needed the bread.

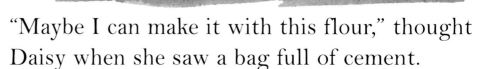

"Maybe I can make it with this flour," thought Daisy when she saw a bag full of cement.

"Perhaps Mr Wolf has never eaten bread and **so he won't know the difference."** Daisy took some cement, mixed it with water and shaped it into a loaf.

Then, as if nothing had happened, she went to Mr W. Wolf's house. When he opened the door, Daisy said, "Mama says thank you. Here's your pan with the delicious doughnuts, lemonade and fresh bread you wanted."

Mr W. Wolf – who by this time
was feeling rather hungry – sat down at the table
and tried one of the doughnuts.
"Uurrrgh!" he said. "How revolting!
This is chicken feed..."
To take the taste away he took a swig from the bottle.
"Pfffst!" he spat. "How revolting!
You've brought me dirty water."
Then he tried the bread:
"Euuuch!" choked Mr Wolf. "How revolting!
You've given me cement to eat."

"You cheated me, so I'll eat you instead!" growled Mr Wolf, and he chased her out of the house. As she ran away he shouted after her, **"Just you wait. Tonight I'll come and get you."**

When Daisy got home she told her mother everything.
Quickly her mother locked all the doors and windows.
"Don't worry," said Mama, "we'll be safe now."
But she had forgotten to block the chimney.
That night, while Daisy tried to sleep, she heard
Mr Wolf howling: **"Here I come! I'm at your house,
and soon I'm going to eat you up!"**

Daisy didn't know what to do.
Mr Wolf climbed on the roof and
howled, "Here I come! I'm on
the roof, and soon I'm going
to eat you up!"
She began to tremble with fear.
Mr Wolf came down the chimney
and shouted: "Here I come! I'm
in the chimney, and soon I'm
going to eat you up!"

"Mama! Mr Wolf is coming!"
shrieked Daisy in terror.
"Quickly, hide under the bed with me!"
cried her mother.
Daisy cleverly left a rag doll in her
place on the pillow and hid under
the bed with her mother.
Mr Wolf came into the little girl's room
and howled: **"Here I come! I'm in
your bedroom, and now I'm going
to eat you up! But where
are you hiding?"** Then he
saw the doll and swallowed
it in one gulp, without
realizing it wasn't a little
girl after all.

Mr Wolf swaggered home very satisfied. He went to bed and slept like a log.

But Daisy's terror gave her such a tummy ache that she had to go to the bathroom five times that night.

She couldn't even feel sorry for herself. Her mother told her a story about another little girl who had actually ended up in a wicked wolf's stomach for doing much less.

Now Daisy doesn't even like sticky doughnuts any more. Just the smell of them brings on a horrible tummy ache, just like that night when Mr Wolf came to eat **her!**